O9-BUB-541

Disney Princess

A Royal Christmas

WRITTEN BY

Lisa Ann Marsoli

ILLUSTRATED BY

The Disney Storybook Artists

Disney PRESS

NEW YORK

Published by Disney Press, an imprint of Disney Book Group.

For information address Disney Press, 114 Fifth Avenue,
New York, New York 10011-5690.

Printed in the United States of America

First Edition

1 3 5 7 9 10 8 6 4 2

G942-9090-6-10196

Library of Congress Cataloging-in-Publication Data

Marsoli, Lisa Ann, 1958-
A Royal Christmas / by Lisa Ann Marsoli ; illustrated by the Disney
Storybook Artists. — 1st ed.
p. cm. — (Disney princess)
ISBN 978-1-4231-3142-7
1. Christmas stories. 2. Children's stories, American. I. Disney
Storybook Artists. II. Little Mermaid (Motion picture) III. Sleeping
Beauty (Motion picture) IV. Cinderella (Motion picture) V. Princess
and the Frog (Motion picture) VI. Title.
PZ7.M356754Roy 2010
[E]—dc22
2009045505

PWC-SFICOC-260
For Text Pages Only

Table of Contents

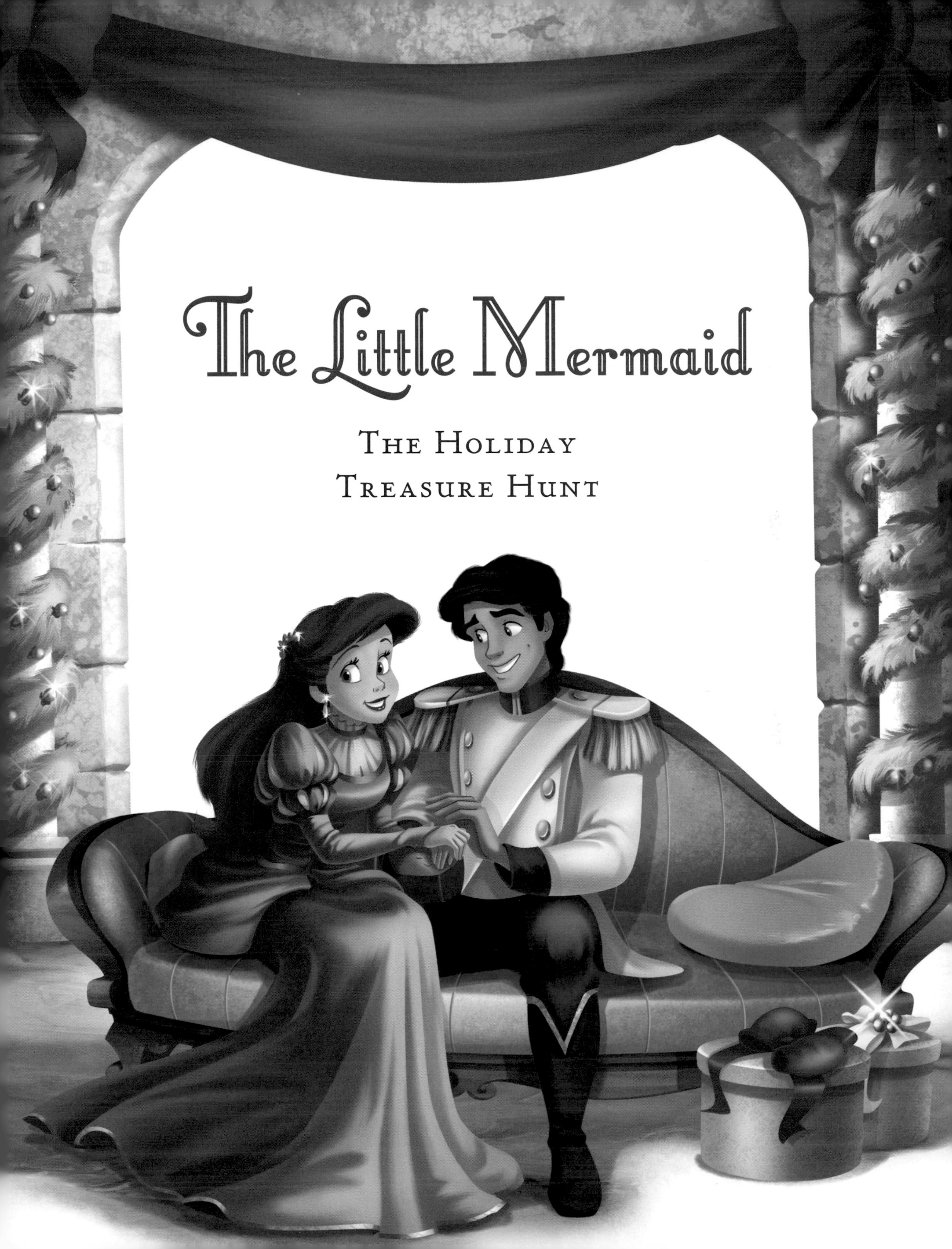
The Little Mermaid
The Holiday
Treasure Hunt

ARIEL AND HER HUSBAND, Prince Eric, were walking along the beach when their dog, Max, ran up. He was carrying a waterlogged boot.

"I've been searching for that boot for months!" cried Eric.

"Burying things and digging them up is his favorite game," said Ariel, shaking her head. At least now she knew what to give Eric for Christmas! But she only had a few days to think of gifts for everyone else.

The prince and princess returned to the castle, where Carlotta the housekeeper announced it was time for tea.

"Already?" asked Grimsby the butler, checking his pocket watch. He gave it a tap. "*Hmm* . . . must be broken."

"Isn't the Christmas tree beautiful?" Ariel remarked. "Carlotta suggested we use red and gold ornaments this year."

"Why, thank you," Carlotta replied. "Those are my favorite colors, you know."

Ariel was delighted. Now she had even more gift ideas.

The next day, Ariel went into town to do her Christmas shopping. She bought Eric a new pair of boots.

For a special surprise, she got him a ship inside a bottle.

Then she chose an elegant pocket watch for Grimsby,

and a gold necklace with a ruby pendant for Carlotta.

Max's present was easy. Ariel stopped at a butcher shop and got the biggest bone she could find!

GIFT SHOPPE

Ariel still had to find gifts for her father, King Triton, her sisters, and her friends from the sea. When she saw a shop window filled with colorful glass hearts, she knew her search was over.

"What beautiful ornaments," Ariel told the shopkeeper. "I'll take them all!"

Back at the castle, Ariel carefully wrapped the gifts and wrote a special message for each member of her family and every one of her friends.

She finished the last note and attached it to King Triton's present.

She placed her father's gift on the pile of wrapped presents, then realized something was missing. It was Max's gift.

Suddenly, Ariel heard a loud chewing noise coming from behind a chair. Max was gnawing happily on the bone she had gotten for him.

"No opening presents early, Max!" Ariel scolded. "Now, shoo!"

Then Ariel hid the wrapped presents under the bed.

On Christmas morning, everyone at the castle shared a festive holiday breakfast.

Afterward, Ariel went to get her gifts, but there was nothing under the bed! So Ariel looked under the rug.

Then she checked inside the closet.

The gifts were nowhere to be found.

"Ariel!" Eric called. "It's time for presents!"

Ariel joined the prince by the tree. "Is it all right if we do that later? I told my merfamily and friends I'd meet them on the beach this morning."

"Of course," replied Eric. "Come along, everyone. We're going on a Christmas visit."

Ariel's friends Flounder, Sebastian, and Scuttle were waiting on the beach.

Scuttle the seagull handed Ariel a small chest. "We thought these *whatchamajinglys* would come in handy!"

Ariel opened the lid and saw the sort of treasures she had loved to collect when she was a mermaid. There was a bent fork and a cracked mirror. "Thank you!"

"We all helped find them," Flounder said proudly.

Just then, King Triton and Ariel's sisters swam up. "Merry Christmas!" they called.

"Merry Christmas!" Ariel replied, waving to her family.

"We brought presents!" Ariel's sister Aquata shouted.

"Oh, thank you!" Ariel exclaimed. "I have gifts for all of you, too, except—"

"*Woof! Woof!*" Max barked. The dog ran up, holding a boot.

"Your present!" Ariel said to Eric. Now she knew where the missing gifts were. Max had buried them!

Ariel quickly said, "Surprise, everyone! We're going on a treasure hunt!"

"Ariel, you are amazing!" Eric said. "Only you could turn the holidays into a new adventure."

Soon, Eric, Carlotta, Max, and Grimsby were digging around on the beach.

Ariel's friends and merfamily cheered them on.

"Try digging near the old rowboat!" Flounder said.

"Or near that sand castle!" Aquata shouted.

Each time a present was found, Scuttle delivered it to its owner.

The treasure hunt was loud, sandy, and the most fun anyone could remember having on Christmas morning.

After the treasure hunt was over, everyone visited at the water's edge. Then it was time to say good-bye, and Ariel, Eric, Carlotta, and Grimsby headed back to the castle.

Later, by the fire, Eric admired his ship in a bottle. "What a wonderful holiday tradition," he told Ariel. "We should have a Christmas treasure hunt every year!"

Ariel just smiled. It had been a day full of surprises, and sometimes the most unexpected treasures were the best.

Sleeping Beauty

Aurora's Homemade Holiday

ONE SNOWY DECEMBER DAY, Princess Aurora and Prince Phillip went for a stroll. The princess was very quiet.

"Is something the matter?" asked Phillip.

"My aunts and I used to love getting ready for Christmas," she replied.

The fairies Flora, Fauna, and Merryweather had secretly raised Aurora to keep her safe from an evil fairy. So she thought of them as her aunts.

"Let's invite them for the holidays," Phillip said.

"What a splendid idea!" cried Aurora.

That afternoon, Aurora and Phillip found a large fir tree to bring back to the castle to decorate. As they rode through a curtain of lacy snowflakes, Aurora sang a carol.

"That's the Christmas spirit!" Phillip exclaimed.

Prince Phillip sent an invitation to Flora, Fauna, and Merryweather. Then he set off on a short trip to attend to some royal duties.

Aurora didn't mind. Now her special Christmas preparations would be a surprise for Phillip when he returned!

When the three good fairies arrived, the princess made her special request.

"You want a Christmas *exactly* like the ones we shared at the cottage?" Flora asked. "That means we can't use magic."

"You'd better take our wands so we're not tempted to use them," Fauna said to Aurora.

The wands were hard to catch. They did not like the idea of being put away!

"Shall we decorate?" asked Aurora. She led the fairies to baskets of evergreen branches, ornaments, and bows.

"Let's start trimming the tree!" exclaimed Merryweather.

"We should hang the evergreen branches first," Flora said.

Waiting for her two aunts to agree could take all day. So Aurora suggested that she and Flora put up the branches while Fauna and Merryweather decorated the tree.

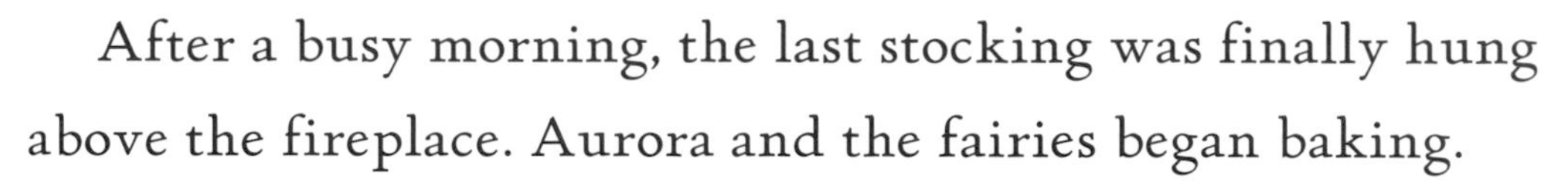

After a busy morning, the last stocking was finally hung above the fireplace. Aurora and the fairies began baking.

"I can't wait until Phillip tastes your special layer cake," said Aurora, "and the rolls with jam inside."

"We'll need lots of red frosting," Flora announced.

"Green frosting is prettier," said Merryweather.

"We'll use both!" Aurora declared.

The next day, it was time to think about gifts. "I want to give Phillip a homemade present," Aurora said. "But what?"

"How about a shirt?" Flora suggested.

"I don't know how to sew," the princess replied.

"We'll show you how," Merryweather said.

Aurora and the fairies spent the day sewing. As Aurora worked on her present for Phillip, she began to smile. "Do you remember the stockings you made when I was a little girl?" she asked.

"Of course!" said Flora. "We forgot to stitch up the bottoms and the gifts fell out."

"You'd say, 'Look, her stocking is empty! We'd better fill it up with more treats!'" Aurora said.

She laughed along with the fairies as they shared their happy memory.

"Oh, dear," said the princess when she looked down at her sewing. "This shirt isn't looking quite right."

Her aunts quickly set aside their projects to help Aurora.

When the preparations were finished, the fairies helped Aurora get ready. Prince Phillip would be home soon.

They made a wreath of holly for her hair. Flora suggested a red dress. Merryweather preferred a blue one. Then Fauna held up a beautiful purple gown. It was perfect!

Flora and Merryweather had to admit the dress looked lovely on the princess.

The last thing Aurora had to do was wrap the prince's gift. Once again, she asked for the fairies' help. When they were finished, the princess placed the present under the tree.

Prince Phillip arrived back at the castle that afternoon.

"Close your eyes," Aurora said, "and don't open them until I tell you to."

She led Phillip into the grand hall where the fairies were waiting. "Ready!" Aurora announced.

Phillip looked around. Crooked wreaths dangled from the walls. The Christmas tree was decorated only on one side. Lopsided cakes, burnt tarts, and misshapen cookies filled a table.

"I've never seen preparations like these before," Phillip said politely. "I can understand why you find them so . . . special."

"Try a lemon tart," said Aurora, holding out a plate to the prince.

Phillip took a bite, and suddenly there was a strange look on his face.

"Oh, dear," Fauna said, "we must have forgotten to put in the sugar!"

Aurora handed Phillip his gift. "One more surprise!"

"A shirt!" said the prince, opening the box.

He put on his present, and the princess and the fairies burst into laughter.

"Oh, dear, that's certainly not the right size," Aurora said.

"Nonsense!" Phillip insisted. "It's a perfect fit."

"Just like you and me," Aurora said to her prince.

Sharing a homemade holiday with Phillip and her aunts had made it the best Christmas Aurora could remember!

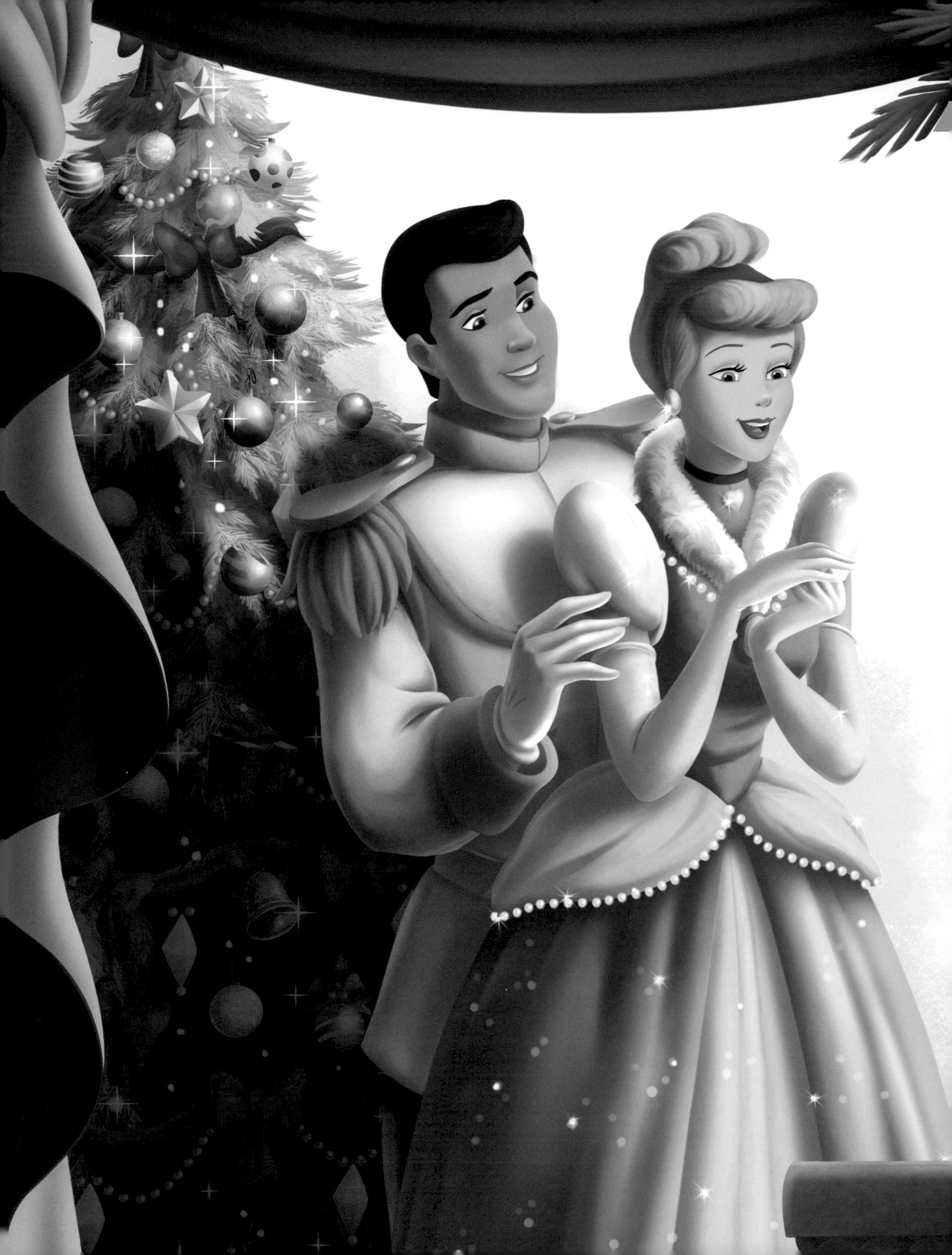

Cinderella

A Perfect Party

CINDERELLA and her prince sat before a roaring fire. It was the beginning of the holiday season, and Cinderella was excited.

"Let's throw a party!" she suggested to the Prince.

"What a splendid idea!" he replied. "How can I help?"

"Just leave everything to me," said Cinderella.

Soon the royal scribes arrived to pen the invitations.

"Thank you, but I'm going to ask everyone in person," Cinderella said, and sent the scribes away.

The next day, the princess began to decorate.

"May we help, Cinderelly?" asked Jaq, who had arrived with Gus.

"Why, of course!" she replied. "Let's start with the grand staircase."

The mice tied a few bows. Suddenly, a spool of ribbon began to unwind, and Gus went rolling down the banister. He didn't mind. It was just like a sleigh ride—without the sleigh!

Cinderella and her mice friends decorated all the large rooms in the castle. Jaq and Gus helped the princess put up evergreen boughs in the ballroom and over the doorways.

Lastly, Cinderella hung stockings by the fireplace—with a little help from Gus.

The only place left to decorate was the stone patio where Cinderella planned to hold her party.

"Won't our guests be chilly out here?" the Prince asked.

"I'm sure it will be fine," Cinderella replied. "Besides, what could be more magical than celebrating under the stars?"

"I like stars. They're twinkly," said Gus as he nibbled on a popcorn garland.

"Gus!" scolded Jaq. "You're supposed to be hanging decorations, not eating them!"

Later, Cinderella went to the royal sewing room. When Prudence, the head of household staff, peeked in, she saw the princess sewing.

"Why don't you ask the royal seamstresses to do that?" suggested Prudence.

"I'm making presents for our guests," said Cinderella.

Christmas Eve finally arrived. The royal chef asked what he should cook.

"Not a thing," Cinderella replied.

Later, Prudence saw her in the storeroom filling baskets with fruit, ears of corn, and different kinds of cheese.

Back on the patio, Cinderella laid out the food.

"*Hmm*," she said. "Something's missing—but what?"

Suddenly, Cinderella's fairy godmother appeared. "My dear, you need a centerpiece." She waved her magic wand and a water pitcher turned into an ice sculpture!

"Now everything is perfect for our holiday picnic," Cinderella exclaimed.

The Fairy Godmother looked at the unusual selection of food. She didn't have the heart to tell Cinderella such a menu would never do for a royal party!

After Cinderella left to change her gown, the Fairy Godmother slipped into the banquet room. "*Bibbidi-bobbidi-boo!*" she said, waving her wand. "Only an elegant party will do!"

Instantly, an elaborate feast appeared. She waved her wand twice more. The court musicians stood ready to play, and there was even an ice sculpture.

"Now, that's better," the Fairy Godmother said.

When Cinderella and the Prince walked past the banquet room, the princess couldn't believe her eyes.

Prudence rushed in. "Where are your guests?"

"My party isn't being held in here," Cinderella told her.

"Then what is?" asked Prudence.

Thinking quickly, the princess said, "A Christmas party in honor of the royal staff. Would you please tell the others?"

"What a wonderful surprise!" said the housekeeper.

Cinderella opened the patio doors. "Merry Christmas!"

A chorus of chirps, barks, and whinnies answered her. All of Cinderella's animal friends had gathered for her party.

"Happy Christmas, Cinderelly!" Gus shouted.

"Merry Christmas," Jaq corrected.

Cinderella's animal friends ate, and then it was time for presents! There were new feedbags, cozy blankets, and stylish mouse-sized outfits. Jaq loved his new jacket so much that he wouldn't stop looking at his reflection.

Later, the Prince and Cinderella danced underneath the stars. When they stopped, they realized they were alone.

"Oh, my! Look!" cried Cinderella. Their animal friends had gone inside and were with the staff. Delighted that everyone was getting along, Cinderella and the Prince joined them.

It was the most unusual Christmas celebration the kingdom had ever seen—and the merriest!

The Princess and the Frog

One Magical Feast

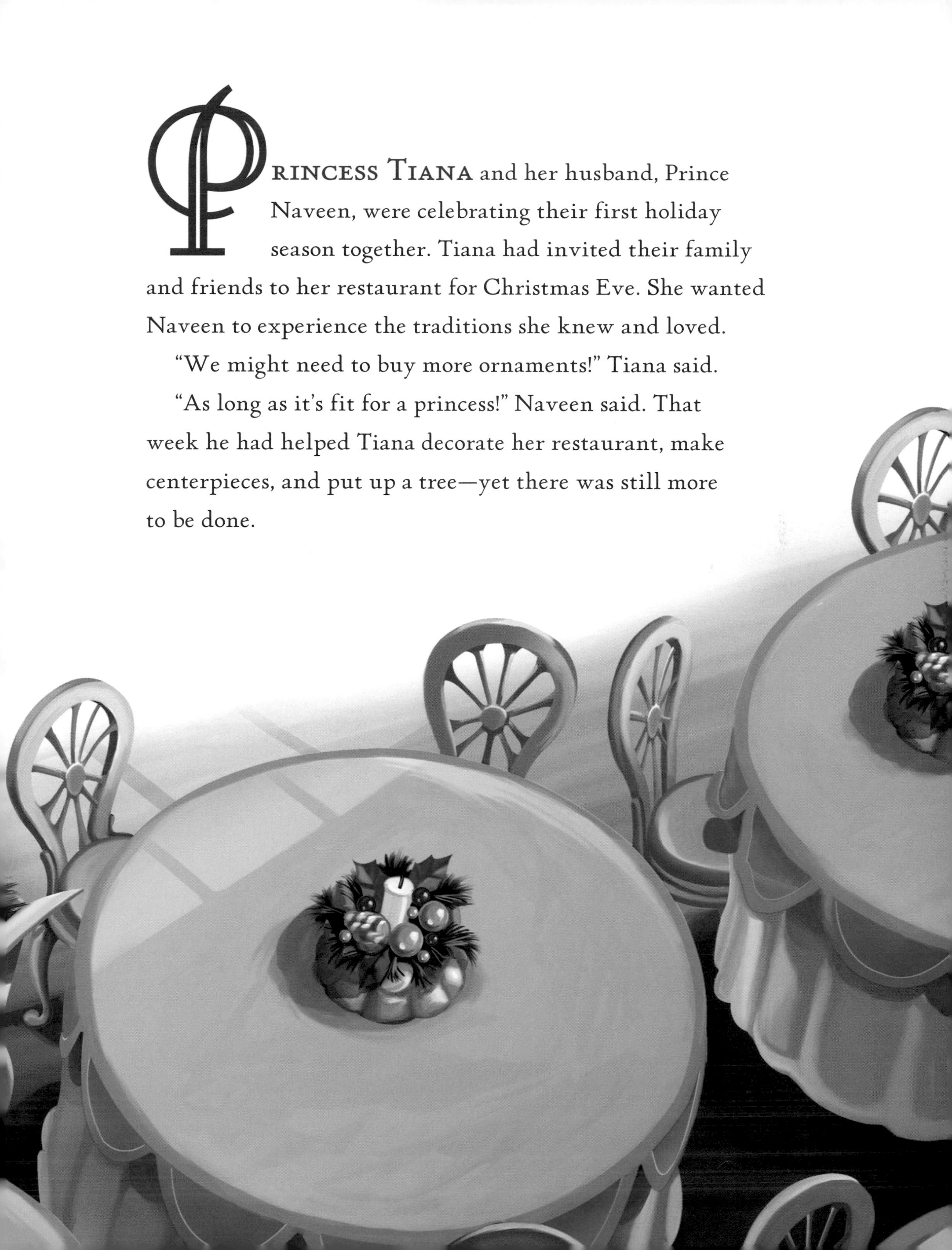

PRINCESS TIANA and her husband, Prince Naveen, were celebrating their first holiday season together. Tiana had invited their family and friends to her restaurant for Christmas Eve. She wanted Naveen to experience the traditions she knew and loved.

"We might need to buy more ornaments!" Tiana said.

"As long as it's fit for a princess!" Naveen said. That week he had helped Tiana decorate her restaurant, make centerpieces, and put up a tree—yet there was still more to be done.

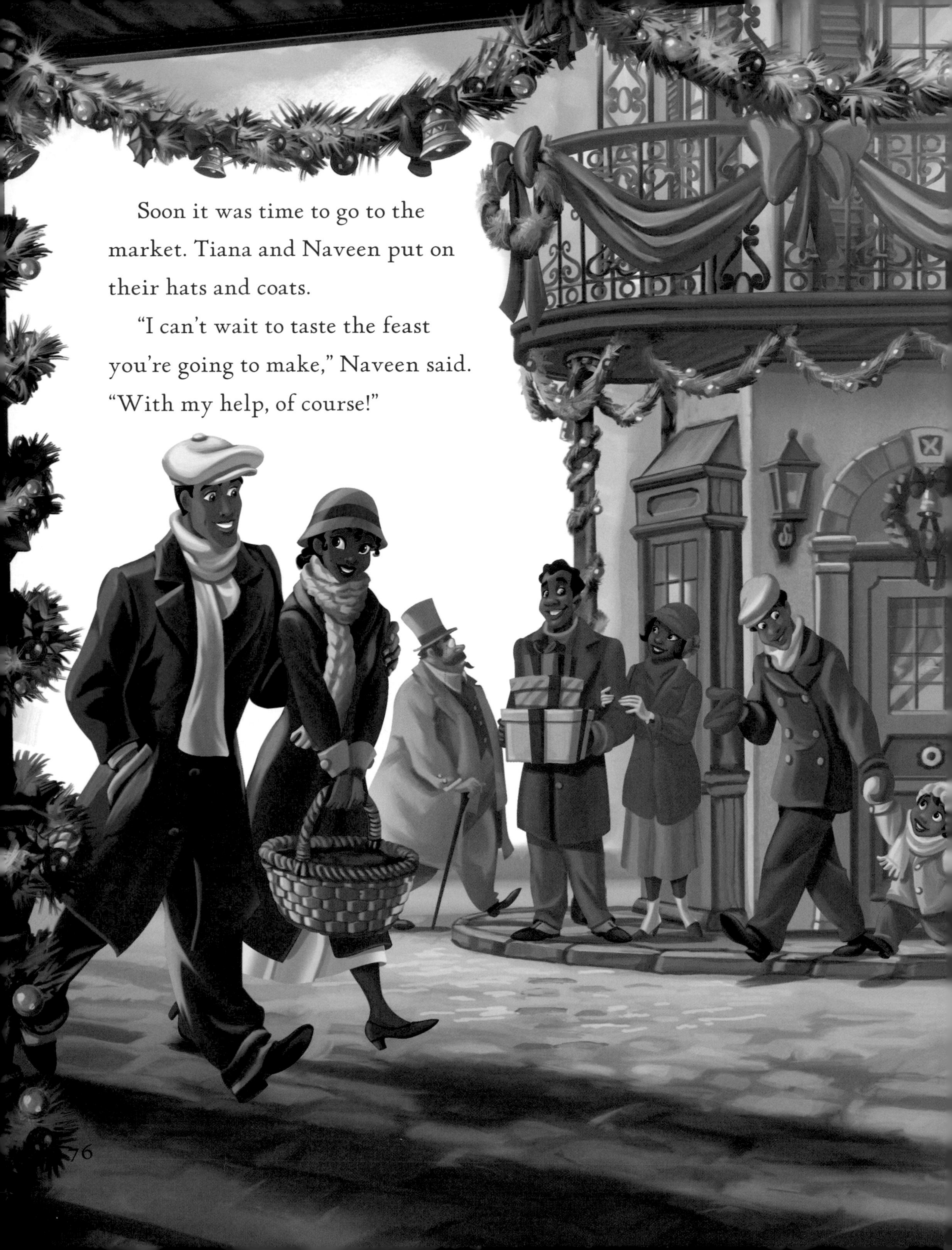

Soon it was time to go to the market. Tiana and Naveen put on their hats and coats.

"I can't wait to taste the feast you're going to make," Naveen said. "With my help, of course!"

"Well, we need quite a few things," Tiana said. "Let's see . . . first we should get the vegetables!"

Next was the butcher shop, then some eggs and cheese. Finally, all Tiana needed was some powdered sugar for her famous beignets.

"I think we'll have to make another trip," said Naveen as he struggled with a tower of parcels. "How many people are we cooking for?"

"My mother, Charlotte, Big Daddy, your parents, and our friends from the town and the bayou. We'll be serving as many people as want to join us," Tiana said happily. "After all, the more the merrier!"

Tiana spent the next few days cooking and baking, with Naveen by her side. Tiana's Palace was open, so Chef Henri was busy cooking all the meals for their customers.

"For someone who didn't know how to chop a mushroom, you've become quite an expert," Tiana told Naveen.

"You've taught me everything I know," Naveen reminded her.

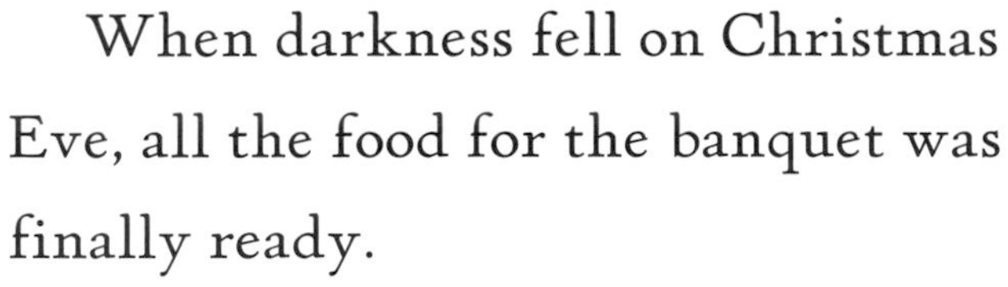

When darkness fell on Christmas Eve, all the food for the banquet was finally ready.

"Before our guests arrive, I have a surprise for you," Tiana announced, handing Naveen his coat.

"Where are we going?" he asked.

"You'll find out soon enough," Tiana answered mysteriously.

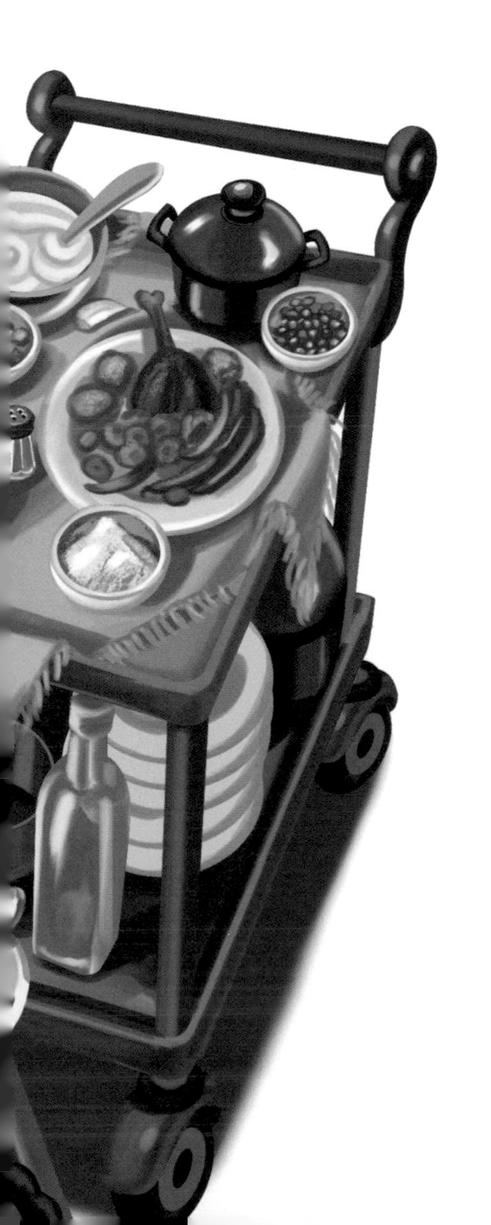

A short while later, Tiana and Naveen paddled a canoe into the bayou. Then Naveen's surprise came into view: huge bonfires lining the river.

"The fires are for Papa Noel," Tiana explained.

"So he can find his way in the sky?" asked Naveen.

Tiana laughed. "Papa Noel doesn't use a sleigh. He travels in a *pirogue,* a flat-bottomed canoe, pulled by alligators."

"I hope he leaves the gators outside when he delivers the presents!" Naveen exclaimed.

Fog rolled in, and Tiana and Naveen paddled toward home. The folks along the river pointed to the couple's canoe. They could see only a red blanket.

"Look!" the river folk shouted. "It's him!" They thought Tiana and Naveen's canoe belonged to Papa Noel!

The people along the river jumped into their boats, hoping to catch a glimpse of the mysterious visitor.

When the bayou folk paddled out of the fog, they found Tiana and Naveen standing on the dock.

"Have you seen Papa Noel?" someone asked.

"We haven't, but since you're in town, would you join us at my restaurant? There's plenty to share!" Tiana said.

"Thank you," said one of the travelers. "I guess we don't mind if we do!"

By the time Tiana and Naveen reached Tiana's Palace, their guests had just started to arrive.

Tiana's alligator friend Louis handed out parcels of sugared fruits and candy.

"It's one of Papa Noel's alligators!" a woman said.

Louis gave her a wide, toothy smile. "Merry Christmas, ma'am!" he said. "I hope you brought your appetite—and your dancing shoes!"

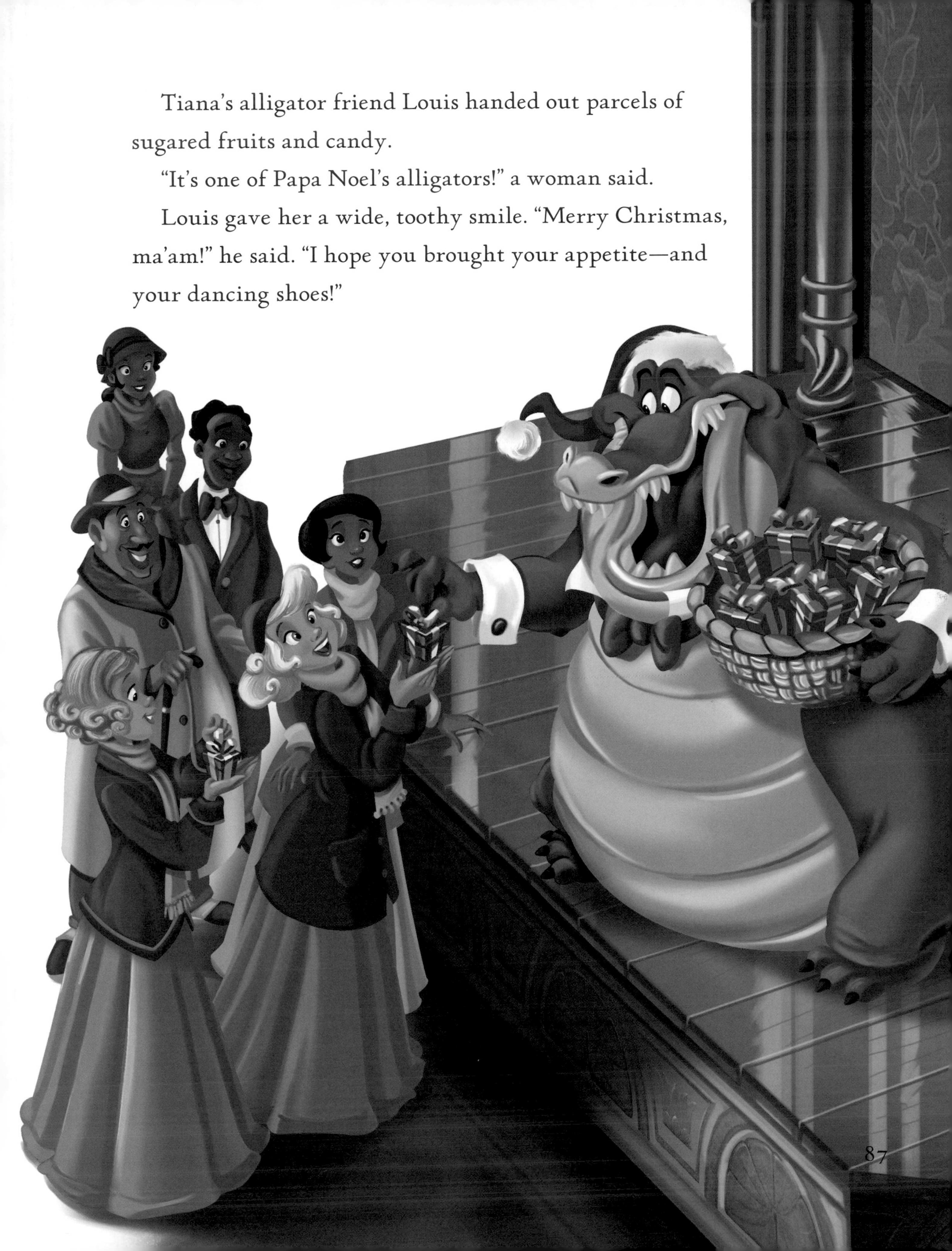

Tiana warmly greeted Naveen's parents and her mother, Eudora. She welcomed her best friend, Charlotte, and her friend's father, Big Daddy LaBouff.

"Some of the guests are saying they saw Papa Noel on the river," Charlotte said. "Do you suppose that's him there?"

Tiana looked up and saw an elderly man in a red suit with the other guests. She was curious, but it was time to go put on her party dress.

Soon, Tiana and Naveen brought out the food.

"Dinner is served!" Tiana announced. On a long table were pots of her delicious gumbo, turkey with chestnuts, roasted ham, grits, yams, vegetables, hominy, and soufflés.

The guests heaped their plates high and dug in. Tiana smiled. There was nothing she liked better than folks enjoying her cooking.

After everyone had eaten, Naveen and Louis played jazzy versions of their favorite Christmas carols. Soon Tiana and her guests were dancing to the music.

Later, Tiana went into the kitchen and filled a cart with custards, cakes, and beignets. The cart was so full that Tiana could barely open the kitchen door.

"Let me help you with that, my dear," said a white-bearded gentleman as he took the cart.

As she ducked back into the kitchen, Tiana realized the man looked just like Papa Noel!

Tiana hurried to the table, but the man had already vanished.

Just then, Naveen walked up. "What a wonderful dinner!" he exclaimed. "The food! The music! The people! It's all so . . ."

"Wonderful? It *is* Christmastime in New Orleans." Then Tiana spotted the man in the red suit. "Do you think that's Papa Noel?"

Before Tiana could investigate, Naveen led her onto the dance floor. "Stranger things have happened," he said.

Tiana grinned. She was delighted that Naveen's first New Orleans Christmas was going so well—for her, that was magic enough.

Louis

The End